D0057023

Dragon Quest

Don't miss the other adventures of Darek and Zantor:

The Dragonling

A Dragon in the Family

Coming soon:

Dragons of Krad

Dragon Trouble

Dragons and Kings

By Jackie French Koller

Illustrated by Judith Mitchell

ALADDIN

New York London Toronto Sydney New Delhi

This book is a work of fiction. Any references to historical events, real people, or real places are used fictitiously. Other names, characters, places, and events are products of the author's imagination, and any resemblance to actual events or places or persons, living or dead, is entirely coincidental.

ALADDIN
An imprint of Simon & Schuster Children's Publishing Division
1230 Avenue of the Americas, New York, New York 10020
This Aladdin hardcover edition December 2018

Also available in an Aladdin paperback edition.

For information about special discounts for bulk purchases, please contact Simon & Schuster Special Sales at 1-866-506-1949 or business@simonandschuster.com.
The Simon & Schuster Speakers Bureau can bring authors to your live event. For more information or to book an event contact the Simon & Schuster Speakers Bureau at 1-866-248-3049 or visit our website at www.simonspeakers.com.
Designed by Laura Lyn DiSiena
The text of this book was set in ITC New Baskerville.
Manufactured in the United States of America 1118 FFG
2 4 6 8 10 9 7 5 3 1
Library of Congress Control Number 2017917589
ISBN 978-1-5344-0068-9 (hc)
ISBN 978-1-5344-0067-2 (pbk)
ISBN 978-1-5344-0069-6 (eBook)

To my brother, Richard, with love

Dragon Quest

Prologue

WHEN DAREK'S FATHER AND BROTHER went off with the other hunters on a dragonquest, Darek wished with all his heart that he could have gone too. Like all the other boys his age, Darek dreamed of being a hero and fighting a dragon. When the hunters returned with a slain Great Blue, the largest and fiercest of all dragons, the villagers gave them all a hero's welcome. Darek thought the hunters were heroes too, until he found a baby dragon hiding in the dead Great Blue's pouch. The dragonling was so small and frightened that Darek felt sorry for it and decided to take it back to the Valley of the Dragons. There, Darek made a startling discovery. Dragons were peace-loving creatures and killed only in self-defense.

Darek gave the baby dragon a powerful name, Zantor, and brought it back to his village. But the other Zorians did not welcome the dragonling. They nearly put Zantor to death, and Darek's father, too! With the help of his best friend, Pola, Darek finally managed to convince the villagers of the truth about dragons, but it was almost too late. The executions had begun! At the last moment, young Zantor proved that he was worthy of his name, saving himself and Darek's father.

Now Darek, Pola, and Zantor are the heroes, and all seems peaceful at last, but Darek's father is still worried. "Such things are not always as simple as they seem," he warns.

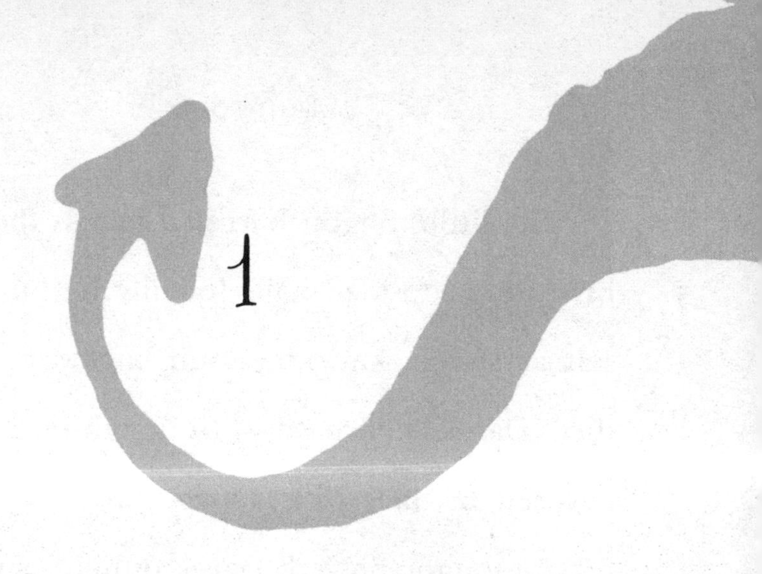

1

DAREK POINTED A STICK TOWARD the sky. He swung it in two wide circles, then slowly lowered it until its point touched the ground. Above his head Zantor soared, following the pattern Darek had traced in the air. The dragonling circled once, then twice over the paddock. Then he swooped down for a landing.

"Hooray!" Darek shouted. He and his best friend, Pola, clapped excitedly. "That was perfect!"

The little dragon barreled across the field in his funny, lopsided gait. Joyfully he hurled himself at Darek, knocking him backward into the dirt. Darek squirmed with laughter as Zantor covered his face with kisses. *Thwip! Thwip!* The forked tongue tickled! Darek pulled a sugar cube from his pocket and tossed it a few feet away. The dragon scuffled after it, and Darek got to his feet and dusted himself off. Pola was laughing, but he wasn't the only one, Darek realized. He turned and saw that he, Pola, and Zantor had an audience. A group of village children were hanging over the paddock fence.

"Zantor! Zantor, come here!" they cried, reaching out eager hands. When Zantor waddled over to play, the children shrieked with delight. "Let me pet him first!" one cried out. "No, me! No, me!" the others shouted.

Darek frowned. He was pleased, of course, that the villagers had finally accepted Zantor. For a time it had seemed that they wouldn't even let him *live.* But Zantor had proven to all that he was both peaceful and courageous, and now they were willing to let him live among them. In fact, Zantor had become so popular lately that Darek seemed to be forever fighting for the dragonling's attention. Darek was the one who had found Zantor, after all, and brought him to the village. Why should he have to share him now with people who hadn't even wanted him at first? It didn't seem fair.

"Hey." Pola nudged Darek in the ribs. "Look who's here."

Darek looked where Pola had nodded. A taller girl had joined the other children. Her long dark hair fell over her shoulders as she reached out and scratched the horn nubs on Zantor's head.

Zantor buried his face in the girl's shining hair and thrummed happily. Darek's frown deepened. "Rowena," he said with a groan.

Pola grinned. "I think she likes you," he said. "She's always hanging around lately."

"It's not me she likes; it's *him,*" Darek said. "Besides, who cares?"

"She's awful pretty," Pola teased.

"Yeah," Darek agreed, "and she's awful headstrong, stuck-up, and spoiled."

Pola laughed. "Maybe you'd be headstrong, stuck-up, and spoiled too if *your* father was Chief Elder."

Darek snorted. Then, as he watched Zantor playing with Rowena, a strange thing began to happen. Happy little thoughts started pushing into Darek's head. They seemed to swell and pop, one after another, like bubbles. For a moment, Darek swore he could smell the perfume of Rowena's hair. He could almost feel the touch of her hands. Then, just as quickly as the funny feelings had come, they were gone. Confused, Darek shook his head.

"What's wrong?" Pola asked.

"I . . . It's weird," Darek said. "I felt like I was inside Zantor's head for a minute."

Pola looked over at Zantor and Rowena and laughed out loud. "Sounds like wishful thinking to me," he said. Then he gave Darek another poke.

Darek's frown returned. If he *had* been inside

Zantor's head, he didn't like what he had felt there. Zantor was growing way too fond of Rowena. "Zantor!" he shouted. "Get back over here."

Rowena wound her arms tightly around the dragon. Zantor glanced over at Darek but didn't try to break free.

"Now!" Darek boomed.

With a sudden jerk Zantor broke away from Rowena. He scuffled over to Darek as fast as his little legs would carry him. Darek looked at Rowena and grinned, as if to say, "See, he's all mine." Rowena glared back, tossing her head.

"I was just petting him," she called. "You don't have to be so mean about it."

"Zantor's not a pet," Darek snapped. "He and I have work to do. If you want to pet something, go pet a yuke."

Rowena glared a moment longer, then turned and stormed away.

Pola looked at Darek and shook his head.

"What's wrong with you?" Darek asked.

"You have a funny way of showing a girl that you like her," Pola said.

"I *don't* like her," Darek insisted. "She's nothing but a pest."

"Oh, yeah?" Pola said. He laughed and pointed to Zantor. The dragonling was still gazing, dreamy-eyed, after Rowena. "Doesn't look like Zantor agrees with you."

2

"YOU SHOULD HAVE SEEN ZANTOR today," Darek said to his mother and father and his brother, Clep, over dinner. "He's learning so fast! He takes off and lands on command. He can fly a circle and a figure eight. . . ."

Hearing his name, Zantor uncurled himself from the hearth. He shuffled over and nuzzled Darek's arm. *"Thrrummm,"* he sang happily at

Darek's elbow. Darek smiled and slipped him a spoonful of barliberry pudding.

Darek's mother, Alayah, attempted to frown.

"No feeding the dragon at the table," she reminded her son.

Darek's father ate quietly. He listened but did not respond to Darek's chatter. Yanek had come to accept Zantor. He even loved the little dragon, but at the same time he had doubts about Darek's dream. A future where people and dragons lived peacefully, side by side, helping each other?

"It's a nice idea," Yanek would say when Darek pressed him about it. "But such things are not always as simple as they seem."

It was true that such things *weren't* simple. Darek had learned that the hard way. When his father had allowed Darek to bring Zantor back to Zoriak, the villagers had been very angry. They had almost burned Yanek at the stake! But Darek and Zantor had proved to the villagers that they were wrong about dragons. One day, Darek was sure, he and Zantor would prove his father wrong about the future, too.

Darek turned toward his big brother. "Hurry and finish eating, Clep," he said. "I want to show you everything Zantor learned today."

Clep was just swallowing his last spoonful of pudding when someone rapped on the door.

"I'll get it," Darek said, jumping up.

He pulled the door open, then stepped back in surprise. "Excellency," he said, bowing low. The Chief Elder himself stood on their doorstep.

Darek's parents and Clep quickly rose to their feet.

His mother rushed forward. “Enter, Sire,” she said. “Please take some supper with us.”

“I have already supped, Alayah,” the Elder said. He nodded stiffly to them all. “I have come to have a word with Yanek.”

“Of course.” Darek’s father bowed and led the way to the front parlor.

Darek and Clep glanced uneasily at each other.

Alayah twisted her apron in her hands. “I hope this visit does not bode ill,” she whispered to her sons.

“As you know,” they overheard the Chief Elder say, “my daughter’s Decanum approaches.”

Darek sighed with relief. So that was all. The Chief Elder had come to talk over the arrangements for Rowena’s Decanum. The whole village was soon to celebrate her tenth birthday. There would be a full parade, a banquet, and a formal ball. Darek's father, as Chief Marksman and Captain of the Guard, would have much to do to prepare.

Darek's mother seemed relieved too. She went back to the table to finish her pudding.

"You know, Darek," she said with a teasing smile, "there has been much talk in the village. Everyonc is wondering who Rowena will choose to be her escort for the Decanum Ball."

Darek's face reddened. Rowena's escort? What was his mother getting at?

"Have *you* any idea who her escort will be?" she asked.

"Not at all," Darek answered shortly.

Clep grinned. "I've heard some names mentioned, Mother," he said. "One very familiar name, in fact." He shot a teasing glance at Darek. "Perhaps that explains the Chief Elder's visit, eh?"

Darek gave Clep such a look of dismay that Clep had to laugh out loud. "It's not the end of the world, little brother," he said. "I can think of fates worse than having to dance with the lovely Rowena."

"Why don't *you* escort her if you think she's so lovely?" Darek snapped. "I think she's a spoiled brat."

"Hush, you two!" Alayah whispered. "Have you forgotten who speaks with your father in the next room?"

Zantor bounced over and butted Darek in the arm. Glad of the interruption, Darek went to the cupboard. He took out the dragonling's bowl and began to prepare his supper.

"It makes no difference what you think,

Darek," Clep said in a more serious voice. "You will, of course, accept if you are asked."

Darek didn't answer. He filled Zantor's bowl with fallow meal and barliberries. Then he ladled warm water over all and stirred it into a mash. The smell of it suddenly made his stomach growl

hungrily. He raised the bowl to his lips and took a big gulp.

"Blaah!" It tasted awful. Darek spit the mash back into the bowl and stared at it. What on Zoriak had possessed him to eat Zantor's food? He'd just finished eating his own dinner! And even if he was hungry, he would never eat fallow meal mash! He looked up and saw Clep and his mother staring at him strangely.

"What *are* you doing?" his mother asked.

Zantor butted Darek's arm again, nearly upsetting the bowl. Darek lowered it slowly to the floor. The dragonling dived eagerly for the food, gulping and gulping. Slowly the hunger pangs in Darek's stomach began to subside.

"I know what he's doing, Mother," Clep said. "He's trying to change the subject."

"What subject?" Darek mumbled, still staring at Zantor. The dish was nearly empty now, and Darek was feeling quite full. A bubble swelled and swelled in his stomach. It wiggled its way up through his chest and burst from his mouth. "Bu-urp!"

"Darek!" his mother exclaimed.

Darek clapped a hand over his mouth. "Sorry," he muttered. What was happening to him?

Clep frowned and shook his head. "Why would anyone want to go to the ball with a dragon-wit like you, anyway?" he asked.

"I'm sure Rowena *doesn't* want to go with me," Darek retorted. "Why do you even listen to those stupid rumors?"

"Ahem."

Darek looked up at the sound of the deep voice. His father's broad frame filled the doorway. He was staring at Darek with a serious look on his face.

"You had better come in here, son," he said. "The Chief Elder's mission today concerns you."

Darek swallowed hard and stared at his father.

"Go on with you," Clep said, grinning broadly and giving Darek a little push toward the parlor. Darek stumbled a few steps, then recovered and followed his father in silence. The Chief Elder stood waiting, tall and stern.

"I've a question to put to you, boy," he said as Darek approached.

Darek's heart sank. He lowered his eyes and nodded. "I . . . I would be honored, Sire," he mumbled.

"Honored?" the Elder repeated. "Honored to do what?"

Darek glanced up at his father and then back at the Elder.

"Why . . . to escort Rowena to the ball, Sire," he said. "Isn't that why you're here?"

The Elder's lips twitched. A glint of humor sparkled in his eyes. "You flatter yourself, son," he said. "My daughter sent me on no such mission."

Darek wanted to faint with relief. The Chief Elder's mission had nothing to do with the Decanum Ball! He wouldn't have to dance with Rowena after all. But then a warm flush of embarrassment crept up his neck. What a fool he had made of himself!

"I'm sorry, Sire," he mumbled. "What is it that you wished to discuss with me?"

The Elder folded his arms across his chest, and his long robes gathered around him. "I want your dragon," he said. "I came to buy Zantor."

3

DAREK'S EYES OPENED WIDE. COULD he have heard right?

"Y-you want to *buy* Zantor?" he stammered.

"Yes." The Chief Elder began to pace. His mood seemed suddenly to turn sour. "I never dreamed I'd allow one of the nasty creatures into my household," he said. "But Rowena has taken a fancy to the beast and will have nothing else. I wouldn't give the matter a second thought if it weren't her

Decanum. One must . . . make allowances at such a time." He rolled his eyes at Darek's father. "You are a father too, Yanek," he said. "I'm sure you can understand."

"Well I do, Sire," Yanek said, nodding.

The Elder stopped pacing and turned to Darek. "Name your price, boy," he said. "And mind you, be fair about it."

Darek's mouth dropped open. "But I *can't* sell Zantor," he said. "I mean, he's not for sale."

The Elder's brows crashed together. "Not for sale?" he boomed. "What do you mean, not for sale? Everything is for sale. Don't be trying to cheat me, boy—driving the price up. I'll have you in the stocks!"

"No, Sire," Darek blurted. "I'm not. It's just that . . . Zantor isn't a *thing*; he's my friend. I

can't sell him. I . . . I don't own him. Dragons can't be *owned.*"

"Barli rot!" the Elder bellowed. "Your father said I must speak to you. Now, name your price and be quick about it!"

Darek glanced at his father and swallowed hard. Then he took a deep breath and bravely returned the Elder's stare. "I . . . I don't own him," he repeated. "He followed me home from the Valley of the Dragons of his own free will. He stays with me because he wants to. He's my friend. That's all."

The Chief Elder's eyes blazed. "Yanek," he said, turning to Darek's father, "I grow weary of your son's impertinence. Name me a price for the beast, and let me be on my way. I've more important matters to attend to."

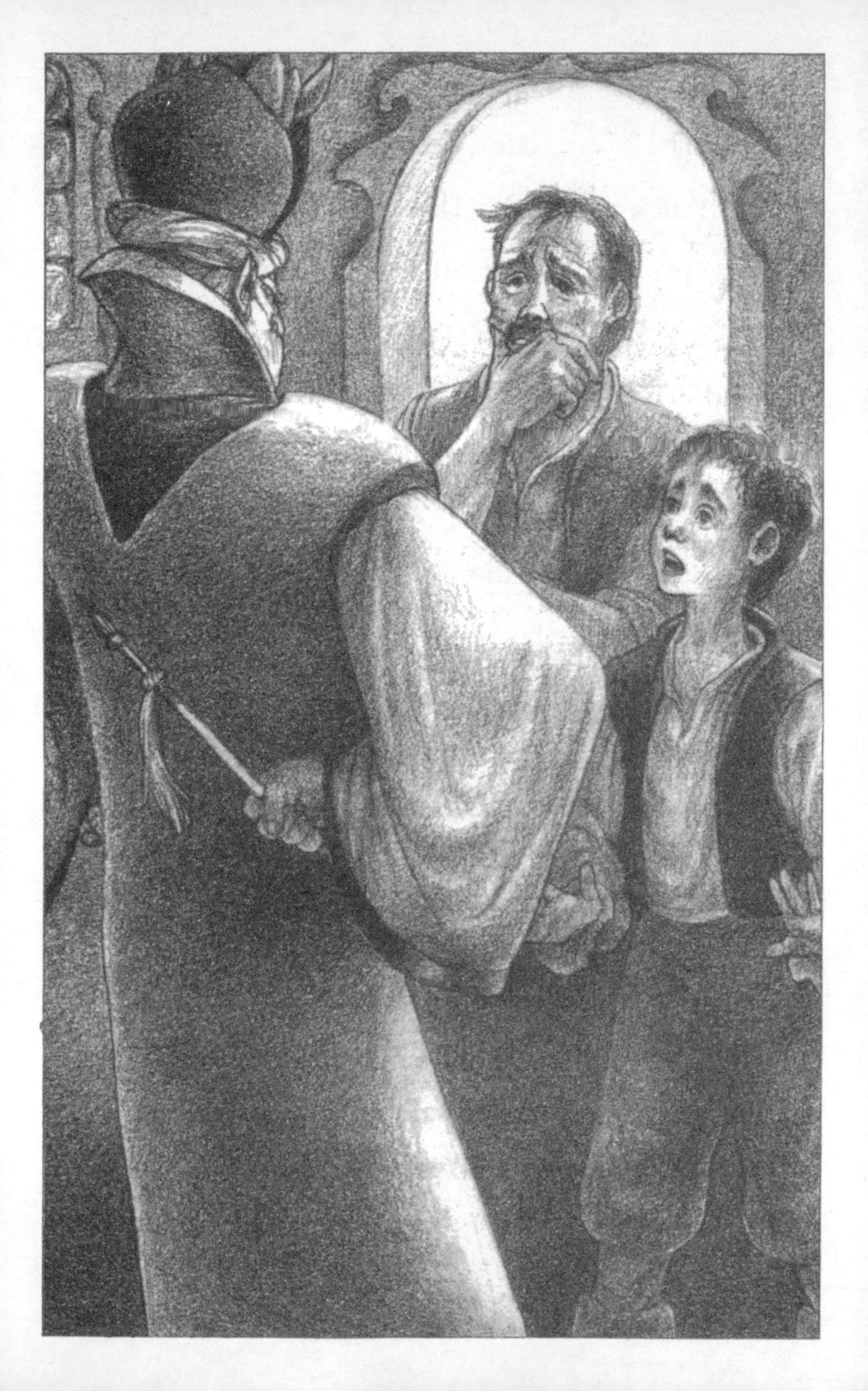

Yanek glanced at Darek. Darek pleaded with his eyes, begging his father to understand. Inside, he could feel himself trembling. He remembered all too well what had happened the last time his father had defied the Chief Elder.

At last, Yanek drew in a deep breath and bowed to the Elder. "My apologies, Sire," he said. "But if my son says the beast is not for sale, I fear it is not for sale."

The Chief Elder's eyes widened, then narrowed down to angry slits. His nostrils flared. "Fine, then," he spat. "In that case, Yanek, you will ready your men for a dragonquest on the morrow. Be prepared to leave at dawn for the Valley of the Dragons. There you will stay until you have captured a dragonling for my daughter's Decanum." He leaned forward and pressed a finger hard into Yanek's chest. "And it had better be a Great Blue!"

With that, the Elder turned and strode from the room, his royal robes billowing out behind him.

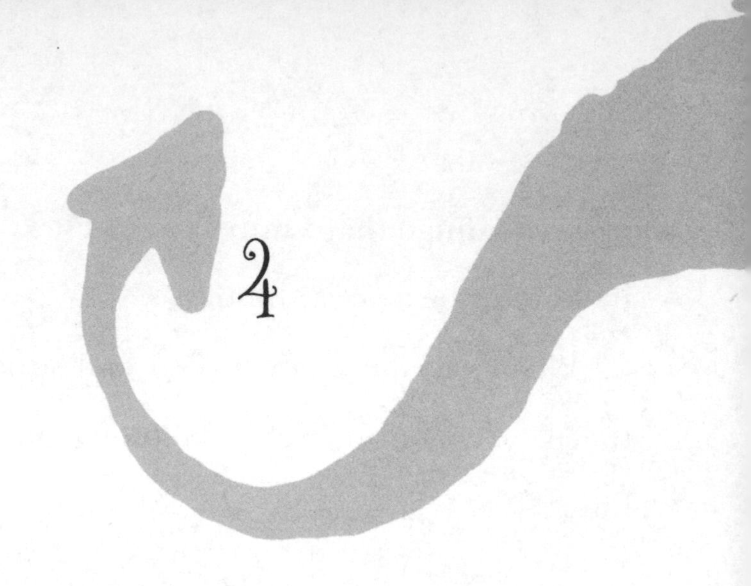

4

DAREK RAN ACROSS THE PADDOCK after his father, tugging at the sleeve of his jerkin. "Please, Father," he begged. "You can't do this. It isn't right."

"Darek," his father said, "I am weary of discussing this with you. The Council of Elders decides what is right and wrong. I am Captain of the Guard. I must follow the orders of the Council."

"But you're an elder yourself," Darek argued.

"With one vote," his father reminded him.

"But you can convince the others. . . ."

Darek's father stopped and stared down at Darek. "Convince them of what? That my son should have a dragon and the Chief Elder's daughter should not?"

"But Zantor chose to be with me. No one *captured* him. It isn't the same," Darek argued.

Yanek shook his head. "I'll do my best to try and prevent bloodshed," he said quietly. "That's all I can promise."

Darek saw the expression in his father's eyes and realized that it was senseless to argue further. Yanek did not approve of this mission either. But nothing would keep him from doing his duty. Darek sighed and nodded. "Can I go along, at least?" he asked.

"I'm sorry," Yanek said. "You're to stay here, with your mother." Then he strode over to where Clep and the others stood waiting in the early morning light.

Yanek gave the order to mount, and the dragon-quest party rode out. Throngs of villagers followed them to the edge of town, cheering and wishing them well. *Just like the old days,* Darek thought, *when the men used to hunt dragons.* Darek had hoped those days were gone forever. Zantor shuffled over to him.

"Rrronk," he cried.

Darek stared sadly at the little dragon. Zantor's own mother had been killed brutally, needlessly, on just such a dragonquest. "I'm sorry, my friend," Darek said quietly.

Suddenly from across the paddock there came a soft call. "Zantor . . . Zantor, come here, fella!"

Zantor's ears pricked up, and Darek whirled around.

Rowena! How dare she come here now?

"Stay," Darek commanded in a low growl, but it was too late. Zantor was already half running, half flying toward the girl. Darek ran after him, but by the time he reached Rowena and the dragon, they were already snuggling together.

"Zantor!" Darek shouted, stomping his foot. "Come here!"

Zantor glanced at Darek but did not pull away. Rowena twined her arms around the little dragon's neck and kissed him on the nose. Zantor looked up at her, his green eyes shining.

"Soon we'll have a new friend!" she told him excitedly. "Another little dragon to play with."

"Thrummmm," Zantor sang happily.

Darek was so angry at Rowena he felt like he could breathe fire.

"A friend!" he spat. "Do you steal a *friend* from its mother, Rowena? Do you tear it from its family? Force it to leave its home? Is that how you treat your *friends*, Rowena?"

Rowena glared at him. "That's what *you* did, isn't it?" she asked innocently.

"You know full well it's not," Darek snapped. "Zantor's mother was dead when I found him. She was killed on a dragonquest. He came with me because he chose to."

Rowena tossed her head. "And my dragon will choose to be with me," she said. Then she hugged Zantor tighter and narrowed her eyes. "Just like Zantor would, if you'd *let* him. Wouldn't you, Zantor?"

Zantor stared at her with adoring eyes. *Thwip!* Out flicked his tongue, planting a kiss on her cheek.

Suddenly all Darek's anger melted, and he felt a rush of tenderness toward Rowena. She seemed to be the sweetest, loveliest creature he had ever seen. Before he knew it, *he* was kissing Rowena on the cheek too!

"What are you *doing*, you dragon-wit!" she shrieked. She gave Darek a shove, and he sprawled on his back in the dirt. He lay there staring at the sky, his head spinning. Did he . . . ? Had he just . . . ? No. He couldn't have. It must have been a dream. He turned and looked. Rowena was gone.

Yeah, that's what it was, he told himself. A terrible, horrible dream. That's all. But . . . then . . . if it *was* just a dream, why did he feel like thrumming?

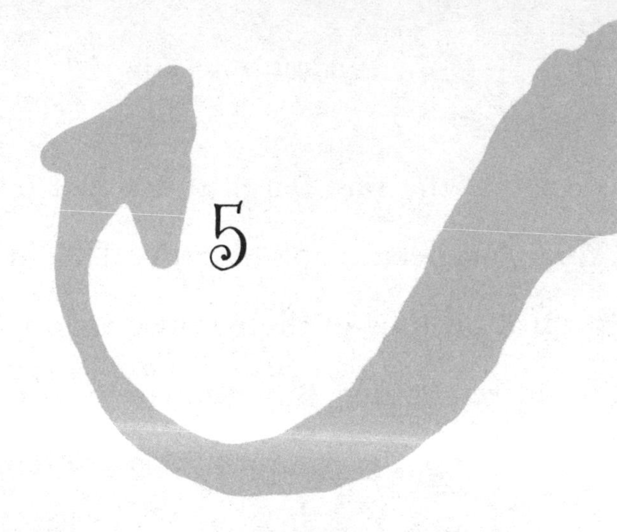

5

DAREK COULDN'T SLEEP. HE WAS TOO confused. And too angry with that . . . girl! She had no idea how much trouble she was causing. She had never been to the Valley of the Dragons. She didn't know how beautiful it was, how majestic the dragons were at peace.

A dragonquest! Darek shuddered at the thought. What did Rowena know of the horrors of battle? Had she ever ached over the loss of a dear one the way Darek still ached over Yoran? Yoran had been Clep's best friend. He'd been like a third brother in their house as long as Darek could remember. But now he was dead. Killed on the last dragonquest, like so many other young men before him. Killed fighting a dragon that only wished to be left alone. Yoran had died fighting Zantor's mother. And she had died too, defending her baby, Zantor. Now other dragons might die. And men, too, maybe even his father or Clep. All for the foolish whim of a spoiled, selfish girl.

Darek sat up and threw his covers aside. At the foot of the bed, Zantor stirred, instantly alert. Darek couldn't stand it any longer—doing nothing. Even now a battle might be raging. He had stopped a battle once. Maybe he could do so again. His father would be angry with him if he disobeyed, but Darek had to follow his heart. He had always followed his heart, and it had not yet led him astray. He dressed quickly and pushed his bedroom window open. Then he motioned for Zantor to come to him.

"Hush," he whispered, pressing a finger to his lips. He stared directly into the little dragon's eyes. How could he explain to Zantor what he wanted him to do? He touched Zantor's chest, then his own, then pointed to the ground, two stories below. "I want you to fly me down there," he said.

Zantor looked out the window and then back at Darek. Goose bumps broke out on Darek's skin as he saw a light dawn in the dragon's eyes. Zantor understood! They were communicating somehow, mind to mind. Darek had little time to ponder this wonder, for Zantor quickly sprang into action. He leaped to the window ledge and fluttered out into the night. Slowly he began to circle, then picked up speed. Darek climbed out and crouched on the windowsill, waiting. He had no doubt that Zantor could do what he'd asked. Small as the dragon was, he was capable of enormous, if brief, bursts of power. Darek had seen him carry things many times his own weight.

Zantor circled twice more, then somehow Darek knew the time was right. Just as Zantor swooped by, Darek leaned forward, and the dragonling plucked him neatly from the ledge. Together they fluttered toward the ground. Zantor's wings pumped mightily as his claws gently grasped Darek's arms.

"You did it!" Darek praised him when they touched down safely. "Good boy."

"Thrummmm, thrummmm," Zantor sang, glowing with pride.

Motioning the dragonling to follow, Darek crept around to the stables. He chose two strong, young yukes and led them outside. They began to fret in the darkness, but he calmed them with sugar cubes and saddled them. He climbed up on one and grabbed the other's reins.

"C'mon, Zantor," he whispered. "Let's go get Pola."

Zantor took to the air and followed at close range.

Pola's bedroom was on the ground floor of his family's home. A light rap on his window quickly

woke him. It took no more than a word from Darek to persuade him to come along. Pola never was one to resist an adventure. He was dressed in an instant, and they were off.

The going was slow at first because of the darkness, but once the sun rose, Darek, Pola, and

Zantor made better time. By midday they had reached the Black Mountains of Krad.

"We're about halfway to the Valley of the Dragons," Darek announced. He eyed the Black Mountains warily as they skirted the smoke-shrouded crags. The trees and grasses on the mountainsides had died long ago. Nothing was visible through the haze but twisted stumps and jagged rocks. "Lord Eternal, those mountains are creepy," Darek said.

Pola nodded, shivering in the shadows of the peaks. "I get the feeling that something—or *someone*—is up there watching," he said. "Don't you?"

Darek laughed. "Kradens?" he asked.

Pola laughed too. Zorian legends told of Kradens, fierce, hairy men who had supposedly driven the Zorians' ancestors out of Krad long ago.

"You don't believe those old myths, do you?" Pola asked.

Darek snorted. "What do you take me for, a nurseling? Of course I don't believe those old wives' tales."

"It's supposed to be true that our ancestors came out of those mountains in the Beginning, though," Pola said.

Darek shrugged. "It's hard to believe anything alive could come out of there," he said.

"They weren't always black and dead," Pola reminded him. "It is said that in the Beginning, they were just as beautiful as the Yellow Mountains of Orr."

Darek stared hard at the forbidding peaks. "If that's true," he wondered aloud, "then what caused them to die?"

"I don't know," Pola said. "But I'd sure like to go up there and try to find out."

Darek whirled to look at his friend. "Are you joking?" he asked. "You know it's forbidden to go up there."

Pola laughed. "Oh, and you never do *anything* forbidden, do you?" he teased. "Might I remind you that we're on a forbidden quest right now?"

"That's different," Darek said.

"Different how?"

Darek turned serious. "People used to go into the Black Mountains in the Long Ago," he said quietly, "but no one ever came back alive. That's why it's forbidden, Pola. Have you forgotten?"

"But nobody's gone in generations," Pola argued. "Maybe things have changed."

"Yeah." Darek nodded toward the mountains.

"For the worse. Only a fool would go up there, Pola."

Pola was quiet for a while. There was no sound but the *clip-clop* of yuke hooves and the rush of wings as Zantor soared overhead. An acrid smell hung in the air, though, a smell like death.

"What if . . . What if the ones who went didn't come back because it's so nice there?" Pola said at last. "What if they didn't come back because they didn't *want* to come back?"

Darek laughed out loud. "Nice?" he said. "Does anything about those mountains look *nice* to you? Besides, if it was so nice, don't you think *someone* would come back and tell the rest of us?"

Pola smiled. "Yeah, I guess you're right," he said. Then he gazed back over his shoulder. "Sure would be a great adventure, though, wouldn't it?"

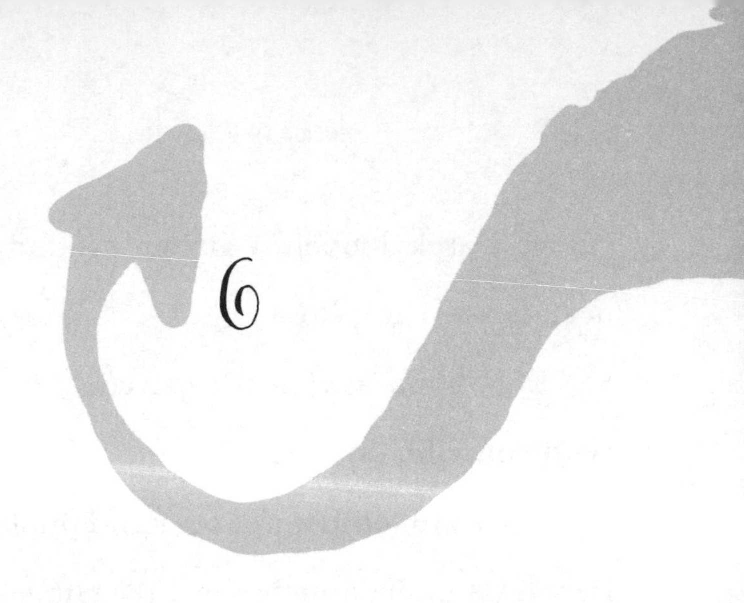

6

DAREK, POLA, AND ZANTOR REACHED the Yellow Mountains of Orr by night. The campfires of the Zorian hunting party flickered on a ridge about halfway up the slopes. Darek and Pola made their own camp well below. To be sure they wouldn't be seen, they went without a campfire. At dawn they skirted the main path and found another way up the peaks, leaving the yukes tied below. Darek looped a halter around Zantor's neck to keep him close.

"Easy, now, easy," he whispered. "This is just to keep you safe, my friend." Zantor did not object. He seemed to sense the danger and put his trust in Darek. Carefully, quietly, the three climbed the last few hundred feet.

"Wow!" Pola exclaimed when they finally reached the top.

"Thrummmm," Zantor sang softly as he gazed once again upon the valley of his birth.

"I told you it was beautiful," Darek whispered.

"I've never seen anything so beautiful in all my life," Pola agreed in a hushed voice.

Everything was peaceful in the valley. Although they had a day's head start, the hunting party had apparently made no move as yet. Darek was not surprised. His father had promised to try to avoid bloodshed. To do so, the hunters would have to lie low and watch the dragons' movements for some time. They would have to wait for just the right moment to sneak in and do their dirty work. Only then would they stand a chance of escaping. Even so, it would not be easy.

The mountains around the valley sparkled. The soft violet rays of the morning sun bathed them in pale hues of blue and rose. Dragons perched on the crags like great colorful blossoms. Others soared in graceful circles through the air. Still others grazed peacefully on the valley floor. Darek saw Yellow Crested dragons, and Green Horned, and also a few small Purple Spotted. The dreaded Red Fanged and Purple Spiked that once struck terror into the hearts of all Zorians were completely

gone. Zorians had hunted them to extinction. It was the Red Fanged and Purple Spiked that had long ago given dragons a bad name, Darek was certain.

"Where are the Blues?" Pola asked.

Darek searched the valley, troubled by this question. "I don't know," he said. "I saw only one female and her three dragonlings when last I came. She lived in that cave high up on the mountainside there." Darek pointed. "I'd hoped there were others, off hunting or something, but I see no Blues again today."

"The Great Blues have been the favored game of the dragonquests ever since the Red Fanged and Purple Spiked disappeared," Pola said. "Can it be that they are nearly extinct now too?"

Darek looked at Zantor and swallowed hard. He had not thought of this before. "I pray not," he said quietly.

Pola gazed thoughtfully out over the valley. "Two males were taken in the dragonquest before last," he said. "They could have been the fathers of Zantor and the other three."

Darek felt a sinking in his heart as he recognized

the likely truth of Pola's words. "Yes," he said quietly. "They could, indeed."

"The other three young ones . . . ," Pola said. "Are they males or females?"

Darek thought back to his earlier trip to the valley. He had spent time in the Great Blue's cave, trying to get her to adopt Zantor. He remembered that the Great Blue's dragonlings had pouches like their mother. "They are females all," he said.

Zantor suddenly sprang upright and started thrumming wildly. Darek tightened his halter and pulled him close.

"Rrronk! Rrronk!" Zantor cried, struggling to get free.

"Shush, shush, Zantor, no!" Darek cried in Zantor's ear. "You have to stay still."

The dragonling quieted, but Darek sensed

his longing as he stared out across the valley.

"Look!" Pola whispered.

So that was what Zantor was so excited about. The Great Blue was emerging from her cave! She unfurled her silvery wings and stretched them out full-length. She stepped to the edge of the cliff and sprang off as lightly as a bird. Out against the sky she soared, blue on blue. The sun glinted and danced on her wings as she circled nearly over their heads.

"She's magnificent," Pola said.

"Thrummmm," Zantor sang, looking up.

"Yes." Darek smiled and rubbed the little dragon's head. "One day you will be just as magnificent, my friend."

One by one, the three smaller Blues appeared at the cave mouth and fluttered out after their

mother. Darek smiled, happy to see that they were all still there and healthy. Then, like a cloud across the sun, a new thought came to him.

"Pola," he whispered, "if what you say is true, then Zantor is the last male Blue alive."

Pola nodded somberly. "And if he doesn't grow up and mate with one of those three," he added, "they will be the last Blues . . . *ever.*"

As if he clearly understood Darek and Pola's words, Zantor looked up at them with mournful eyes. "*Rrronk,*" he cried softly.

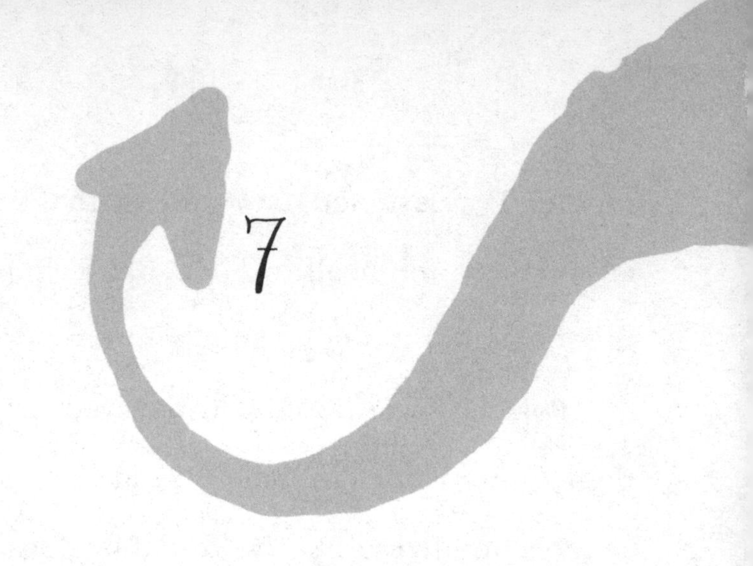

7

NOTHING MOVED ON THE RIDGE through all the long, hot day. Pola went back to the yukes to get the waterskins, then took Zantor with him in search of food and fresh water. He returned with an assortment of nuts and berries and the two bulging skins. Darek drank deeply and squirted a little of the refreshing liquid over his sun-scorched head. Zantor curled up to sleep in the shade of an outcropping of rock. As the

afternoon dragged on, Darek and Pola dozed too.

"Do you think the hunting party will try anything today?" Pola asked when they woke.

Darek stretched and looked at the sky. "I don't know," he said. "If they do, it should be soon. The dragons will be waking from their afternoon naps shortly."

"Why is that a good time?" Pola asked.

"The adults wake first," Darek explained. "They go off to forage for dinner while their little ones are still asleep."

"But how will our men capture a dragonling without causing a ruckus?" Pola asked.

Darek shook his head. That he didn't know. He feared to think what might happen if things went wrong. Dragons were peaceful if left alone, but they were fierce and dangerous when threatened.

Their fiery breath and razor-sharp claws had sent many a Zorian to an early death. Darek prayed to Lord Eternal that his father had a plan.

True to Darek's words, the adult dragons soon began emerging from their caves and drifting down into the valley. Before long, the Great Blue appeared. She flew to the valley's far end and disappeared into the thick forest. Sadly Darek watched her go. She had no idea of the danger threatening her young ones.

Darek still clearly remembered his first meeting with her. She had been ready to defend her babies with her very life. She was a mother, after all, as loving as any human mother. He didn't like to think of the pain and loss she must suffer now because of Rowena. New anger at the girl flared inside him as he watched the mouth of the cave.

The little ones were in there, probably still sleeping, just as Zantor still snored beneath his rock. If the hunting party planned to act today, now would be the time.

"Look!" Pola whispered. He pointed to the ridge above the cave.

For a moment Darek couldn't believe what he saw there. Another Great Blue had appeared! It was a male, small for a Blue, but definitely full-grown. The shape of the head and the color of the scales were unmistakable. As Darek and Pola watched, the new dragon started to move down the mountain face. But something was wrong. It didn't have an adult dragon's strong, high-stepping gait. Instead it moved in a sluggish, awkward fashion, almost as if it were dragging itself.

"Lord Eternal!" Darek whispered. "It's a decoy!"

He and Pola stared at each other in astonishment. "They must have made it from one of the dragon-skin hangings in Elder Hall," Pola said.

Darek smiled and shook his head in wonderment. What a wise man his father was!

"Do you think it could possibly work?" Pola asked.

Darek felt torn as he watched the awkward creature lurch into the mouth of the cave. He'd been against the whole quest from the start, and his heart wanted it to fail. But his head knew that lives were on the line, including his father's and Clep's. If this plan didn't work, there would surely be bloodshed and death before the day was over. He grabbed Pola's arm and squeezed tight. "Pray," he whispered.

***

Not one, but all three little dragons followed the strange new Blue out of their cave and up over the ridge. Darek and Pola moved around the mountain, closer to the hunting party's encampment, to get a better look. Zantor had awakened, and Darek was having trouble controlling him.

"Easy, fella, easy," Darek whispered. "I know you want to go to them, but you can't just now."

"Rrronk," the dragonling replied.

The odd procession was coming closer and closer, making its way down the back side of the mountain. Strange emotions tumbled through Darek's mind as Zantor thrummed and tugged on his halter.

"Easy," Darek repeated, but he now felt drawn to the procession too. The need to be with the other dragons was becoming an ache inside him.

He found himself itching to let Zantor go.

"Here," he said, handing the halter to Pola. "You'd better hold him. I'm not sure I can trust myself."

Pola looked at him strangely. "Trust yourself to do what?"

"I feel like I'm inside Zantor's head again," Darek said.

Pola arched an eyebrow. "What are you talking about?"

Darek shook his head. "I'll explain later," he said. "Just hold him—tight."

Pola took the tether and wrapped it tightly around his wrist. Zantor's head sagged, and Darek felt the dragonling's disappointment as keenly as if it were his own. He turned away and tried to concentrate on the procession.

"Do you think they're going to take all three?" Pola asked.

"I'm afraid they'll have to now," Darek said. "If they try to separate them, there'll be a ruckus for sure. And that would bring the mother in no time."

"Won't she follow anyway?" Pola asked.

"Not for a while," Darek said. "The dragonlings are old enough to forage for themselves. She probably won't miss them until nightfall when they don't return to the cave." A picture of the distressed mother dragon flashed into Darek's mind. She would be so worried about her young ones. If only there were some way to stop this cruel quest.

"But nightfall is only four or five hours away," Pola said.

Darek shrugged. "That's all the head start the hunting party can hope for," he said. "That, and the chance that it will take her a while to pick up the trail. It's all rock up on the mountain, so there won't be footprints, and dragons don't have much sense of smell."

"Maybe she *won't* pick up the trail," Pola said hopefully. "Maybe she'll think they're lost in the valley somewhere."

"Maybe," Darek said, but he was doubtful.

Suddenly Zantor gave a quick twist, yanking the halter free. With a sharp cry of glee, he took to the air and zoomed straight toward the dragon procession.

"Hooray!" Darek shouted, leaping joyfully into the air. Then he crouched down and clapped his hand over his mouth.

Pola stared at him. "Have you taken leave of your senses?" he asked. "What are you yelling about? The hunting party heard you for sure!"

"I know, I know," Darek said. "I'm sorry. That wasn't me shouting. It was . . . Zantor, sort of."

Pola narrowed his eyes. "Did you get sunstroke up there today?" he asked.

Darek shook his head. "No. At least, I don't think so. Something else is going on. Something is happening in my mind. I don't understand either, but we don't have time to worry about it right now."

Pola sighed and stared at the fleeing dragon. "That's for sure," he said. "As soon as your father sees Zantor, he'll know for sure that we're here. What are we going to do?"

Darek thought about facing his father and the others and swallowed nervously. "You can go home," he said to Pola. "They won't know you

were with me. This was all my idea, anyway. I'll . . . take the blame."

Pola stared at him a long time, then walked over to his yuke and climbed into the saddle.

"See you back home," Darek said quietly.

"No you won't," Pola said. He leaned forward and handed the reins of the other yuke to Darek. Then he smiled. "An adventure's an adventure, all the way to the end," he said. "I'm with you, my friend."

Darek smiled and hoisted himself up into the saddle. He reached out to Pola, and they clasped arms in a Brotherhood shake.

8

DAREK'S FATHER'S EYES WERE STERN. "I don't care what your reason is!" he boomed. "You disobeyed an order, and you will pay the price when we return home."

"Yes, sir." Darek bowed humbly. "I'm sorry, sir."

"Aargh!" Darek's father stomped off. "Get out of my way. I've more important things to worry about."

Darek went back and stood beside Pola. They were silent for a while, watching the dragon procession. Darek felt awful, standing there, doing nothing, as the dragonlings walked into a trap. Then an idea began to take shape in his mind. If he could get close to the dragonlings, he might be able to free them. They would fly straight back to their mother. Maybe then the men would give up this foolish quest rather than risk a direct confrontation. It was a long shot. But if Darek didn't do something soon, it would be too late. He approached his father once more.

"Father," he said hesitantly. "I . . . think maybe I can help."

"Out of my sight, I told you!" his father bellowed.

Darek took a step back, but then Clep came up and put a hand on Darek's shoulder. "Wait a moment," Clep said. Then he turned to Yanek.

"A word with you, Father?" Clep asked.

Yanek stared at his two sons a long moment. Then he and Clep stepped to one side and put their heads together. Their voices rose and fell. Darek strained to catch snatches of their conversation.

"Way with dragons . . . ," he heard Clep say.

"Disobedient whelp . . . ," his father replied.

"Understands them . . . ," Clep said.

"Taught a lesson . . . ," his father grumbled.

As Darek watched his father and brother argue, his own feelings warred within him. Clep was standing up for him, taking his side. How could he let his brother down and free the dragons now? And what would the elders do to his father if Darek made trouble again?

"Out of time . . . ," he heard Clep say at last. Both Clep and Yanek turned then and looked toward the mountain. The party of dragons, now including Zantor, would soon have to be dealt with.

Yanek swore under his breath and looked over at Darek. "Do you think you can get close to those beasts without spooking them?" he asked.

"Yes, Father."

"Can you get tethers on them?"

Of this Darek wasn't so sure, but one thing he did know. "If anyone can, Father," he said, "I can."

"Well enough, then," Yanek said. "I'll settle my score with you later. Take the tethers and go."

"Yes, sir." Darek looked over at Pola, and Pola smiled back. He raised his arm and clenched his hand into a fist, palm forward. It was a Brotherhood fist. *Lord Eternal go with you,* it meant. Pola understood. He knew Darek had a difficult choice to make, and he was offering his support, no matter what Darek decided. Darek nodded his thanks to his friend. Then he started for the dragons. But what should he do? Free them or capture them?

"Son."

Darek stopped and turned. His father and Clep stood side by side. Both raised their fists as well. They trusted him, Darek realized. He felt a warm pride inside. Then, one by one, the other hunters in the party raised their Brotherhood fists too. Darek swallowed hard. He couldn't let them down. Not now. Besides, what if he freed the dragons and the men did decide to go after them again? The capture might not go so smoothly next time.

He wasn't being a traitor to Zantor and the dragons, Darek told himself as he started up the mountain. He was just doing his best to see that no one, dragon or Zorian, got hurt.

9

DAREK DIDN'T KNOW WHY THE LITTLE dragons seemed so glad to see him. Did they remember him from his earlier visit to their cave, or did they take their cue from Zantor, who greeted him with nuzzles and thrums? Either way, they welcomed him eagerly into their rollicking reunion with Zantor.

When Darek offered them sugar cubes, they gobbled them up and followed after him, begging for more. They were suspicious of the tethers at first, but Darek had a plan. He slipped a tether on and off Zantor, giving him a sugar cube reward each time. Before long, the other three dragons were wearing tethers and munching on sugar cubes too.

Soon all four dragons slept in a contented

little heap in the back of a wagon pulled by Darek and Pola on their yukes. Night had fallen, and they guided the yukes carefully along a path lit only by Zoriak's twin moons. Behind them, in two columns, rode the rest of the hunting party.

Darek was glad things were going so well, but he still couldn't help worrying. It was all too easy. Much too easy. He kept watching over his shoulder for the Great Blue.

"Maybe she doesn't care," Pola said hopefully. "Maybe the dragonlings are old enough to be on their own now. Maybe she's ready to let them go."

"Maybe," Darek said. This didn't seem likely, but he *was* surprised that they had made it all the way back to the Black Mountains without any sign of the angry mother. Maybe Pola was right. Maybe he was worrying for nothing. He settled back in the saddle and allowed himself a small sigh of relief.

And then he heard it.

The shriek, though far off, sent chills up his spine. "She's coming," he whispered.

The hunting party had heard it too.

"Circle up!" Darek heard his father shout.

The two columns behind Darek and Pola split and arched out around them. Soon the boys and the dragonlings were enclosed in a great circle.

"Now what?" Pola asked.

"Battle," Darek said bitterly. "Didn't you know it would come to this?"

The Great Blue shrieked again, closer this time. With cries of alarm the dragonlings awoke. Darek could feel Zantor's fear. He hastily tossed some sugar cubes back into the wagon, trying to keep them all calm.

"GRRRAWWWK! GRRRAWWWK!"

The ground around them shook as the Great Blue thundered out of the sky, swooping down almost on top of her young ones.

"Rrronk! Rrronk!" the dragonlings cried, straining at their tethers.

Darek's and Pola's yukes danced and bucked.

"Control your mounts!" Darek's father shouted. "Prepare for battle. Shields up, bows ready!"

"GRRRAWWWK!" The Great Blue swooped again, this time letting loose a blast of flame. The little ones shrieked, and Darek's yuke reared up on its hind legs. Pola's yuke spooked and reared too. Then, at the same time, both yukes bolted. The wagon lurched after them, bouncing over the rough ground.

"Eeeiiieee! Eeeiiieee!" the little dragonlings

screamed. Their cries seemed to whip the yukes into a frenzy. Darek and Pola fought for control of the reins, but there was no holding the frightened animals back. Their hooves thundered, tearing up the ground and bathing them all in a cloud of dust.

"Get out of the way!" Darek shouted as the wagon bore down on the battle circle. Men and yukes scattered as the wagon broke through. Behind them Darek and Pola could hear the great dragon scream as she charged once more. Sounds of a battle raged as the wagon continued to barrel out of control. It was headed straight for the Black Mountains of Krad! Fear roared in Darek's ears. His own terror, and Zantor's, too, blocked out all thought.

The wagon jounced over the foothills as the

runaway yukes started up the mountain pass. Clouds of black smoke loomed ahead. The acrid smell stung Darek's nose. There was no escape. They were headed straight into the Mountains of No Return!

"Jump!" Darek shrieked to Pola as the first ghostly wisps of smoke began to drift past them. "Jump!"

At the last moment Darek threw his reins aside and jumped. He landed with a thud and rolled over and over, coming to rest at last against a rock. He looked up just in time to see the runaway wagon and the four little dragons disappearing into the black, smoky haze.

And then he saw something else. A figure still sat astride one of the yukes!

"Pola!" Darek shrieked. *"Pola, jump!"*

But Pola didn't jump. Instead he raised his arm high, his hand clenched in a Brotherhood fist.

"An adventure's an adventure!" he shouted.

And then they were gone. . . . Pola, Zantor, all of them. Vanished.

Darek got to his feet and ran a short way into the mist. "Pola! Zantor!" he cried. But there was no answer. No sound. Darek's eyes watered, and his nose stung. He turned and staggered out of the mist again. Tears streamed down his cheeks. He turned once more and stared in stunned disbelief at the spot where the wagon had disappeared. Minutes passed. Maybe even hours. Darek didn't know. He felt empty inside, drained, as if nothing was left of his heart but an aching hole.

Then, just as dawn broke, there was a horrible, agonized cry, and the battle sounds in the distance ceased. Darek turned slowly, and the ache inside him deepened. There, on the ground, surrounded by the hunters, lay the Great Blue. The soft rays of the morning sun peeked over the mountains and glinted off her bent and lifeless wings.

10

DAREK RUBBED HIS HAND ACROSS THE top of Pola's Memory Stone. In time, maybe, he would be able to come here to the Memory Place and think warm thoughts, the way he did when he and Clep visited Yoran's Memory Stone. But now all he felt was pain.

If only Zantor were still here to comfort him, to make him smile with his silly dragon antics. But Zantor was gone too. Gone forever, along with

Pola and the other three dragonlings. The Zorians would never know another Great Blue. Darek sighed deeply. Sadness seemed to fill every corner of his mind and body, leaving no room for anything else. He slowly rose to his feet and started toward home.

"Darek?"

The voice startled him and caught him unaware. He turned, and when he saw who had spoken, his sorrow turned to something darker. Darek had never hated before, but he hated now.

"I . . . I've been waiting for a chance to speak with you," Rowena said.

Darek stared straight ahead, not trusting himself to speak.

"I . . . I want to tell you that I'm sorry," she went on. "That I . . ."

"Sorry!" Darek whirled now and faced her. "You're *sorry*?" He spat the words like fire. "You're *sorry* that my two best friends in the world are dead?"

"They're not . . . dead," Rowena said, her eyes glassy with tears. "They're just . . . gone."

Darek glared at her. "How do you know they're not dead?" he asked. "Besides, what difference does it make? I'll never see Pola or Zantor again. Pola's parents will never see their son again." He turned and gazed off into the sky, off toward the Yellow Mountains of Orr. "And no Zorian from this day forward will ever again see the beauty of a Great Blue," he added softly.

"I know. . . ." Rowena's voice was almost a sob. "I'm sorry," she repeated. "What more can I say?"

Darek spun around angrily. "You're *sorry,* all right," he said in a low snarl. "You're just about the sorriest excuse for a Zorian I've ever laid eyes on." Then he turned and strode away.

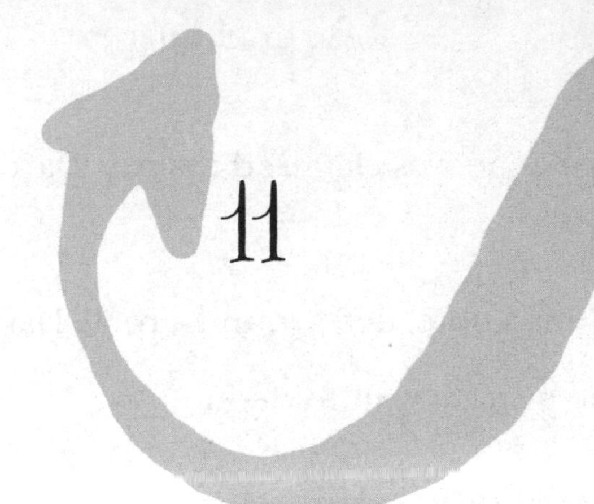

11

DAREK TOSSED AND TURNED. ANOTHER sleepless night. He sat up and stared off toward the Black Mountains of Krad. Where were Pola and Zantor? he wondered. How were they? Were they dead or alive? Outside he heard the clatter of yuke hooves and wondered who might be passing by at this late hour. Then something flew in through the open window and landed at the foot of his bed.

The yuke hooves clattered away as Darek reached down.

It was a note, tied around a rock. Darek yanked off the twine and unfolded it.

“They are gone, not dead,” it said. “I know this. Don’t ask me to explain how. But I do know. And where there is life, there is hope. I ride tonight for the Black Mountains, there to undo the wrong I’ve done.”

Darek stared at the note for a long moment until its meaning finally sank in. Rowena was heading out on a quest to find Pola and the dragons.

“Zatz!” he cried. “That fool girl!”

He pulled on his boots and his jerkin, then dashed through the sleeping house and out to the barn. He saddled the fastest yuke in the herd and flung himself onto its back. Out into the night he rode, faster and harder than he'd ever ridden before. Wind filled his mouth and tore at his hair. The yuke's hooves flew over the moon-silvered ground, tearing up league after league. At last the Black Mountains loomed closer. Overhead the sky grew pale with the approach of dawn.

As he bore down on the mountains, Darek spied a figure up ahead. Her loosened hair streamed wildly out behind her. Rowena and her yuke moved as one, smoothly gliding over the landscape. Darek frowned. She sat a good yuke; he had to grant her that. He spurred his yuke harder in an effort to close the gap between them, but his yuke was winded. Overtaking the girl before she reached the pass would not be easy.

"Rowena!" he screamed. *"Rowena, stop!"* But his words only blew back into his own mouth.

Rowena did not stop or even slow when she reached the foothills. On she raced toward the mist-shrouded peaks.

The acrid, dead smell of the mountains made Darek's breath catch in his throat. He was running out of time. He reached back and pulled his yuke's tether rope from behind his saddle. He fiddled with the noose until it was the right size. Then he stood in the stirrups, swung the rope overhead a few times, and let it fly.

"Uumph!" Rowena landed on the ground with a thud. Her frightened yuke clattered off into the foothills.

"You dragon-wit!" she screamed as Darek approached. "What do you think you're doing?"

"Saving your foolish hide," Darek yelled. "Have you taken leave of your senses?"

"What is it to you?" Rowena cried. She got to her feet and slapped angrily at her dust-caked clothes.

"Are you hurt?" Darek asked.

"No, I am not hurt—no thanks to you!" Rowena turned and stomped away.

"Where are you going?" Darek shouted.

"I told you where I'm going."

"Oh, no you're not!"

"Oh, yes I am!"

Darek slid down off his yuke, ran up behind Rowena, and grabbed her arm. "No you're not," he repeated. "You've caused enough trouble already. . . ."

"Me!" Rowena whirled around. "And I suppose you're Sir Innocent, huh? At least *I* have the guts to admit when *I'm* wrong."

Darek stared at her. "What are you talking about?" he asked. "What did I do?"

"What *didn't* you do is more the question!" Rowena said. She pulled free and started up the mountain again. Darek ran after her once more.

"I'm listening, okay?" he said. "How is any of this my fault?"

Rowena glared at him. "If you must know the truth," she said, "I never even wanted a dragon of my own. All I wanted was a chance to spend a little time with Zantor, to play with him now and then. But you were too selfish to allow that. You were too jealous, because you knew he liked me as much as you!"

Darek's mouth dropped open. He tried to think of some sharp words to fling back at her, but he could not.

Rowena stopped walking and faced him squarely. "Did you really think you could keep Zantor all to yourself?" she asked. "You proved to us all how wonderful he was, then you shut us out. Did you really think that was fair?"

Darek tore his eyes from Rowena's and looked down at the ground. Her words stung like the blade of a finely honed knife. And their aim was just as deadly true. He *had* been selfish and jealous. If he'd been willing to share . . .

Darek's shoulders sagged, and his arms fell limply at his sides as the truth became painfully clear. If he had been a little more considerate, Zantor and Pola might still be there.

"You're right," he said softly. "It *is* my fault. Pola . . . Zantor . . . everything."

There was a long silence, and then Rowena put

a hand on his shoulder. “No,” she said. “I can’t let you take all the blame. I was jealous of you too. And I behaved like a spoiled child. We are both to blame.”

Darek looked up, surprised. This was a new side of Rowena, a side he had to respect. “It took guts for you to admit that,” he said.

Rowena smiled and added quietly, “You’ve got guts too.”

“Maybe we’ve been wrong about each other, huh?” Darek said.

Rowena nodded. “Maybe.”

It wasn’t customary to offer a Brotherhood shake to a girl, but somehow it felt like the right thing to do. Darek reached out his arm. “What do you say we start over?” he asked. “Friends?”

“Friends,” Rowena said. She clasped his arm

and gave it a hearty shake. They smiled into each other's eyes for a moment. Then Rowena looked away. "Well," she said, "I'd better get going."

"Going where?" Darek asked.

"There." Rowena pointed into the mist.

"What?" Darek couldn't believe his ears. "You're not still going!"

"I am."

"But . . . it's forbidden," Darek said.

Rowena smiled again. "That's never stopped *you* from doing what you want," she said.

Darek shook his head. Why did everybody keep throwing that back at him?

"The things I did were important . . . ," he started to say.

Rowena raised her eyebrows. "And rescuing Pola and Zantor isn't?"

Darek sighed. "Rowena," he said, "we don't even know if they're alive."

"They *are* alive," Rowena insisted. "I know."

Darek stared at her for a long moment. "Why do you keep saying that?" he asked. "*How* do you know?"

A blush of crimson stained Rowena's cheeks.

"Because," she said, lowering her eyes, "Zantor . . . told me."

"Wh-what?" Darek stammered. A chill crept up his back.

"He . . . speaks to me," Rowena went on, "in my mind."

The chill spread out to Darek's fingers and toes. He sat down on the ground with a thud.

"I know you don't believe me—" Rowena began.

"No," Darek interrupted. He looked up at her and nodded slowly. "I do."

"You do?"

"Yes." Darek licked his lips. "He speaks to me, too."

Rowena's eyes widened. "He does? Really?"

"Yes." Darek nodded again.

"Then you've heard it!" Rowena exclaimed.

"Heard it? Heard what?"

Rowena dropped to her knees beside Darek and stared into his eyes. "Listen!"

For the first time in days, Darek pushed the heavy weight of sadness aside and opened his heart and mind. He listened, quietly, to the thoughts in his head. And then, quite clearly, he heard it! It came faintly at first, then stronger.

"Rrronk! Rrronk! RRRONK!"

"It *is* him," Darek whispered.

Rowena nodded.

Images started crowding into Darek's head. Dragons. Lots of dragons. The other Blues were there, and Pola, too!

"They're all together!" he shouted. "They're alive!"

Rowena smiled and nodded again.

"But where?" Darek asked. "Where?"

"Up there, somewhere," Rowena said, pointing into the mist again. Then she turned back to Darek. "And I intend to find them. Are you with me?"

Darek sat a moment longer, letting it all sink in. Then he got to his feet and stared once more at the bleak mist-shrouded crags. Pola's last words rang in his memory: *An adventure's an adventure!*

"All the way to the end," Darek added softly. Then he turned to Rowena and smiled.

"Yes," he said. "I'm with you, my friend."

Turn the page for a peek at the next book in the series:

Dragons of Krad

1

DARK MISTS SWIRLED AROUND DAREK as he made his way up a narrow pass into the Black Mountains of Krad. Rowena, daughter of the Zorian Chief Elder, followed a few steps behind. The mist felt damp against Darek's skin, and the stench of it made him gag. It smelled like rotted burning flesh, and that worried him.

Darek heard a cough and looked back over his shoulder.

"Are you all right?" he asked.

"Yes." Rowena nodded. "I'm getting tired, though. My eyes sting, and it's hard to breathe."

"Shall we rest awhile?" Darek asked.

"No. Pola and Zantor may be in danger. We've got to keep going."

Darek nodded. He could hear the mind cries, too. His dragon friend, Zantor, was sending messages of distress. Zantor and Darek's best friend, Pola, had disappeared into the Black Mountains more than a week ago. They and three other Great Blue dragonlings had been carried off by a runaway wagon. Darek and Rowena felt responsible. They had been jealous of each other and had quarreled over Zantor. As a result, the Chief Elder had ordered his men to capture another dragonling for Rowena. While on the dragon quest, Pola, Zantor, and the others had been lost.

Rowena coughed again and gasped for air.

"Pull your collar up over your mouth and nose," Darek said. "The cloth will filter some of the smoke."

Strange shapes loomed out of the mist. Black rocks, like cinders, dotted their path. All of Darek's senses were alert, keen to the dangers that might assail them at any moment.

"I wonder what our families will think when they wake this morning and find us gone," he said quietly.

Rowena didn't answer right away.

"We must not think of that," she said at last. "We must dream of the day when we return with Pola and the dragons."

Darek wished he could be sure that day would

come, but he could not. No one had ever returned from the Black Mountains of Krad. For centuries now, it had been forbidden even to venture into them. What would his parents and his older brother, Clep, think when they realized where he had gone? He could see his mother's tearstained face now.

We will find a way back, Mother, he promised silently.

"Did you hear that?" Rowena suddenly cried out.

Darek stopped and listened. He thought he heard a soft scuffling sound, but when he peered into the mist, all he could make out were strange, twisted rock forms and the stumps of long-dead trees. "I don't see anything," he whispered.

"No," Rowena said. "I guess not." She put her

hand to her forehead and moaned softly. "Ooohh," she said. "My head and stomach ache."

Darek's head hurt too. Could the very mists be poisonous? he wondered.

"We're almost to the peak," he told Rowena. "It will be easier going down the other side. We won't have to breathe as hard."

The ground beneath them leveled off at long last, and they started to descend. Darek began to move with greater caution. If something or someone was waiting below, he wanted to see it before it saw him. His headache was worse, making it harder and harder to think. Behind him, he heard Rowena moan once more.

"Are you sure you're all right?" he asked again.

"Yes," she said, but her voice trembled.

Darek's worry deepened. He had to get her

out of the mountains quickly. "Can you walk any faster?" he asked.

"I—I don't know. I can't even think straight."

Darek turned. Rowena's skin was very pale, and her lips looked blue.

"Lean on me," he said.

Rowena gladly took his arm, and they struggled on together. Darek shook his head. It felt as if the mist were seeping into his mind. Minutes seemed to drag by. Rowena was leaning on him more and more heavily.

"Is it much farther?" she asked weakly.

"No, not much. See, the mist is thinning."

"Good, because I don't feel . . . ooohh." Rowena suddenly pushed Darek aside, clapped a hand over her mouth, and started to run.

Darek stumbled on a cinder and fell. "Rowena,

wait!" he cried. He scrambled to his feet again, but before he could catch her, Rowena disappeared into the mist

"Rowena!" he called, but there was no reply, only a distant retching sound.

Then, suddenly, there was a scream.

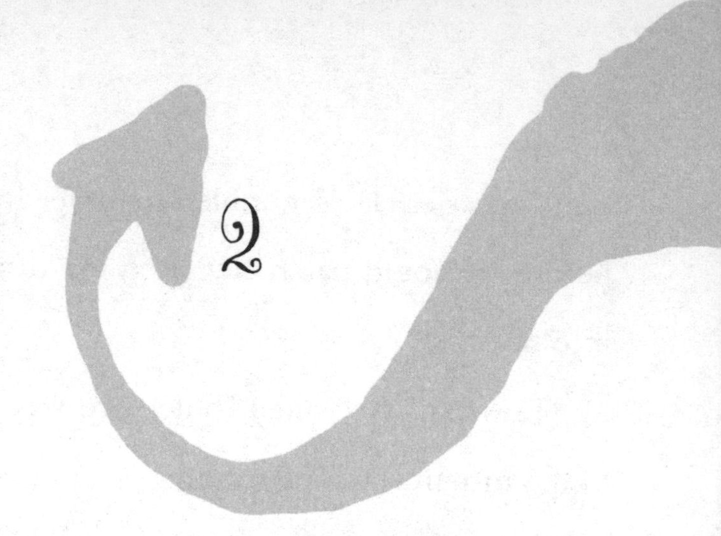

2

DAREK FOUGHT THE URGE TO RUN in the direction of the scream. Instead, he moved cautiously, stealing from rock to rock. If someone, or something, had caught Rowena, he had to be careful. It would do neither of them any good if he got captured too. The mist had cleared a little, and he could begin to see something of Krad. It was a bleak, colorless place, with runty, withered trees and stubby brown grasses.

A movement below caught his eye, and he strained to see.

Rowena!

His friend had reached the plateau at the foot of the mountains. There she was surrounded by a number of bent little creatures that hopped about her excitedly. They were chanting over and over in high, flutelike voices.

"A pretty!" they cried. "A pretty! A pretty!"

Rowena hugged her arms around her like a frightened child. "Go away! Go away!" she cried. "Leave me alone!"

Before long, there was another sound—hooves pounding in the distance. Darek looked toward the horizon and saw a group of riders thunder up over the lip of the plateau. The riders were broad and tall, with dark, hooded capes. They were mounted on long-haired white yukes, much like the ones back in Zoriak, only larger. As the riders bore down on Rowena, the little bent creatures around her shrieked and scurried away.

One of the smaller ones was too slow. A whip lashed out from the hand of one of the riders and stung it a fierce blow on the leg. The creature yelped and scrabbled into the brush. The rider threw his head back and laughed. His hood fell away, and Darek saw a face that was humanlike but covered in fur.

A Kraden!

A chill crept up Darek's back. Back in Zoriak, he had heard stories of Kradens—big, hairy men who had supposedly driven the Zorians out of Krad long ago. Darek had always thought they were just old tales. But these Kradens were real—living and breathing! Poor Rowena looked terrified.

"Who are you?" one of the Kradens demanded.

"Rowena," she answered in a trembling voice.

"Why have you come here?" the man asked.

Rowena seemed at a loss to answer.

Darek felt confused too. Why *had* they come there? Had the mist addled his mind? Why couldn't he remember?

Then he heard a sound deep inside his head. *Rrronk!* Yes! Zantor. Zantor and Pola. That was why they had come. He must keep focused on that.

Rowena must have heard the mind cry too. "My friends!" she said suddenly. "They're in trouble. I've come to help them."

"Have you, now?" The men looked at one another and chuckled. "And how is a slip of a girl like you going to help anyone?"

Rowena drew herself up and tossed her head. "I'm stronger than I look," she announced.

At this, all the men burst out laughing.

"That's good news," one of them said, "because we've plenty of work for you to do."

Rowena crossed her arms. "Work?" she said. "I'll not work for you. I'm the daughter of the Chief Elder."

"Are you, now?" another Kraden said. "Well, then, we'll have to find you a jewel-handled broom, won't we?"

With another loud laugh, the Kradens swooped forward, and one of them scooped Rowena up, pulling her into his saddle.

"Come, lads," he said. "Let's take *Her Highness* to visit old Jazee." Then he and the others turned their yukes around and thundered away.

Darek stared after them. Who was old Jazee? he wondered. And what did the man mean when he said there was plenty of work to do? It did not bode well.

Darek decided to try to keep his own presence a secret until he could learn more. Slowly, he crept down the mountainside until he reached the place where Rowena had been captured. He noticed a trail of dark droplets among the footprints and remembered the small creatures and the lash of the whip. Suddenly, he heard a high, thin cry.

"Gleeep. Gleeep."

Darek's head jerked around. The wounded creature was lying beside a nearby rock, nursing its leg. It caught sight of him and scrambled to get away, but it was only able to move a few steps before collapsing again.

“Gellp!” it cried.

Darek frowned. He had no time to help a wounded . . . whatever. He started to walk away, but his conscience would not let him. Quickly, he pulled his shirt out of his britches and tore a strip from the hem. Then he unfastened the waterskin from his belt and squirted a little into the dirt at his feet, mixing a muddy paste. Taking a handful of the paste, he approached the creature. It shrank back, staring at him with huge yellow-green eyes.

“I won’t hurt you,” Darek soothed. “I just want to help.” He knelt beside the creature and gently straightened its leg.

“Gellp!” it cried again.

“Sorry,” Darek said. “This should make you feel better.” The creature was the size of a young child, with scaly gray skin. It looked almost like a cross between a dragon and a human. Darek couldn't help feeling kindly toward it. He packed the healing mud over the wound, then gently bandaged the leg.

"There," Darek said, getting to his feet again. "If you stay off it for a day or two, you should be fine."

The creature turned and pointed a knobby finger toward the road. "Your pretty?" it asked.

Darek looked down the road, too. There was no sign of Rowena or the men now. "No," he answered. "She's not my pretty. But she's my friend. Do you know where they've taken her?"

"Zahr take pretty," the creature said.

"Zahr?" Darek said. "Who's Zahr?"

The creature gave a little cough. "Zahr, king," it said hoarsely.

Darek stared again at the empty road. “Where did Zahr take pretty?” he asked.

“Slave camp,” the creature said.

Darek whirled around. “Slave camp! What do you mean, slave camp?”

The creature cringed. “Go now,” it said, scrambling away.

“No, wait.” Darek took a breath to calm himself. “Please tell me more about the slave camp,” he pleaded.

The creature coughed again. “Go now,” it repeated. And then, almost magically, it disappeared.

“Hey, wait!” Darek called after it. “One more question, please! Have you seen another Zorian, like me, or a small blue dragon?”

“Zahhhr,” came the faint, choked reply.